Starry Safari

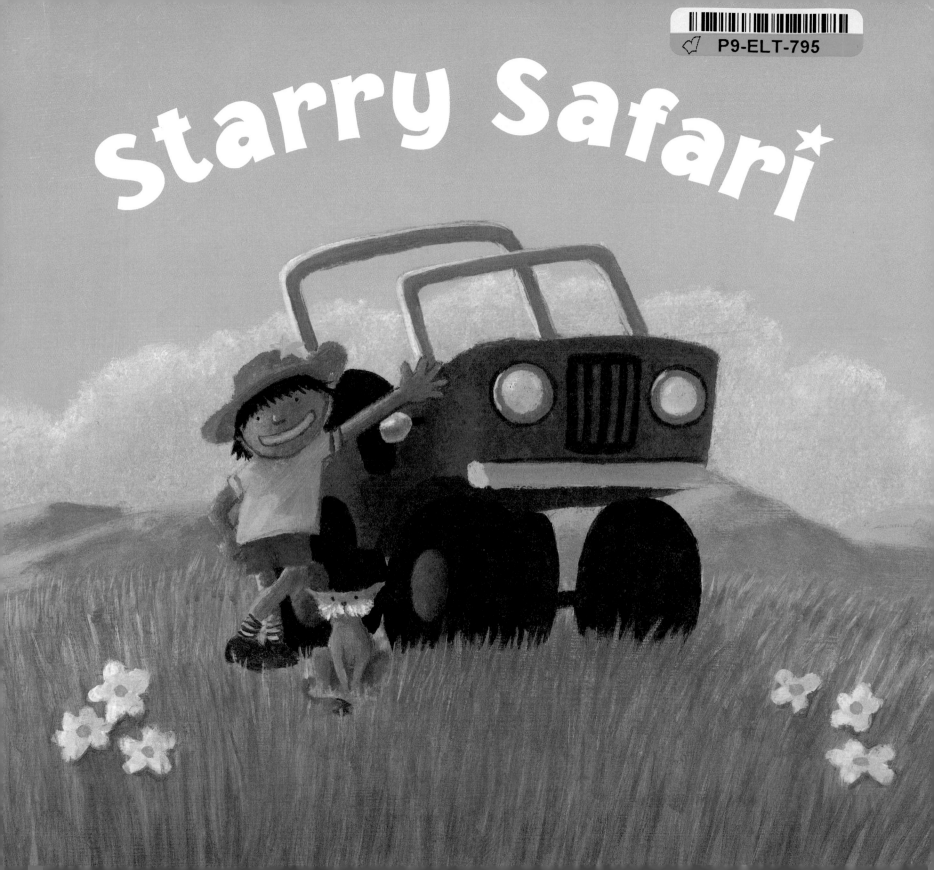

Starry Safari

Linda Ashman   Illustrated by **Jeff Mack**

SCHOLASTIC INC.
New York Toronto London Auckland Sydney
Mexico City New Delhi Hong Kong Buenos Aires

For Sarah, Rachel, Lauren, Daniel, and Steven
—L. A.

To Michael David Fox, artist, teacher, professional humorist
—J. M.

ISBN-13: 978-0-545-10919-2
ISBN-10: 0-545-10919-1

Text copyright © 2005 by Linda Ashman.
Illustrations copyright © 2005 by Jeffrey M. Mack.
All rights reserved. Published by Scholastic Inc., 557 Broadway, New York, NY 10012, by arrangement with Houghton Mifflin Harcourt Publishing Company. SCHOLASTIC and associated logos are trademarks and/or registered trademarks of Scholastic Inc.

12 11 10 9 8 7 6 5 4 3 2 1   8 9 10 11 12 13/0

Printed in the U.S.A.   08

First Scholastic printing, September 2008

The illustrations in this book were painted in acrylics on 140 lb. Arches Aquarelle Watercolor paper.
The display type was set in Jacoby ICG.
The text type was set in Plantin.
Designed by Suzanne Fridley

Racing in my sturdy jeep—
on safari!

Beep! Beep!
Beep!

Passing fields where zebras feast.

Trailing herds of wildebeest.

Gazing at a **tall** giraffe, bump into a rhino calf.

Angry rhino starts to chase.

Lanky ostrich joins the race.

Floor the jeep, and go, go, go!

A roadblock! Buffalo!

Detour! Take the river path.

Join some hippos for a bath.

A wily crocodile!

Somersault with chimpanzees.

Swing with monkeys overhead.

I help gorillas make their bed.

Find a clearing.
Pitch a tent,
assisted by an elephant.
Crawl inside and
curl up tight.

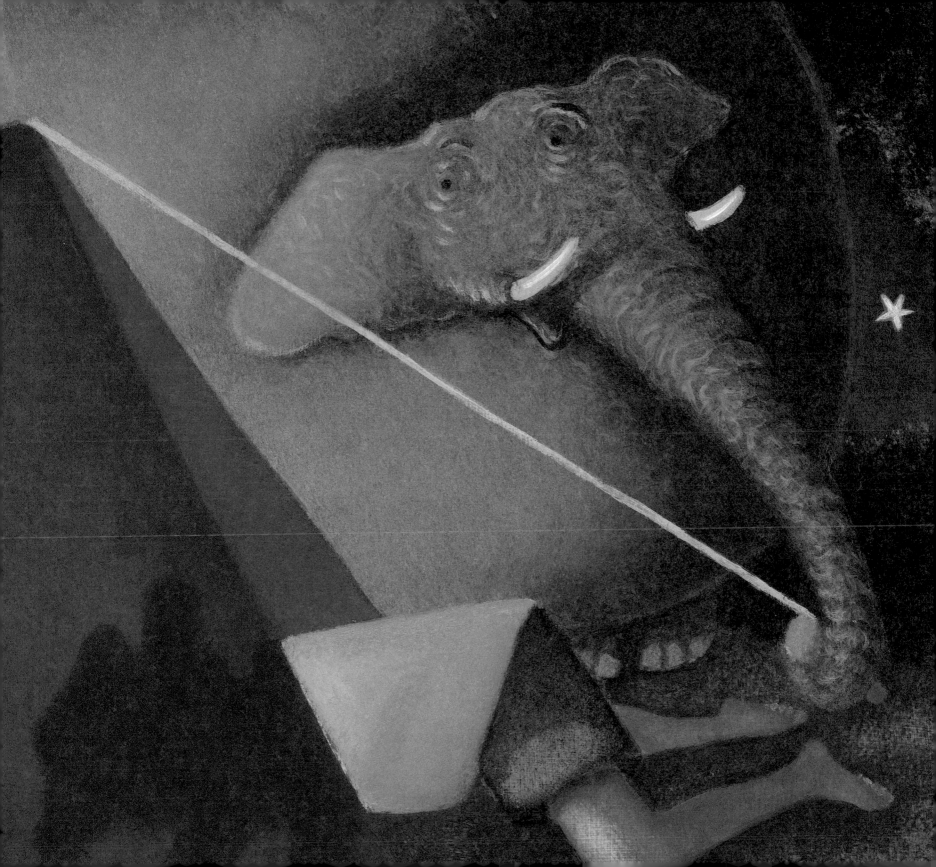

Listen to the noisy night:

HOOT

Snort

Grunt

Growl

Shuffle

Scuffle

Whimper

HOWL

Scratch

Snore

Hisssss

Squeal

Whistle

Rumble

Rustle

A lion! Circling round.
It pounces.
CRASH!
My tent falls down.

ROAR!!! He's ready to attack.

Uh-oh. Footsteps. Greater danger! It's the **Big Safari Ranger.**

Finds me hiding.
Counts to ten.

Then tucks me into bed...again.